Bea and Mr. Jones

Story and Pictures by Amy Schwartz

BRADBURY PRESS   NEW YORK

Bradbury Press, An Affiliate of Macmillan, Inc., 866 Third Avenue, New York, NY 10022. Collier Macmillan Canada, Inc. Manufactured in the United States of America. First Edition.

15   14   13   12   11   10   9   8   7

Library of Congress Cataloging in Publication Data
Schwartz, Amy. Bea and Mr. Jones.
Summary: Tired of kindergarten, Bea Jones trades "jobs" with her father, who works in an office.
    [1. School stories.   2. Work—Fiction]
I. Title
PZ7.S406Be   [E]   81-18031
ISBN 0-02-781430-0   AACR2

For my parents

"I've had it with kindergarten!" Bea Jones said to her father as he was sitting down to breakfast.

"I've had it with beanbag games!

"I've had it with clothespin games!

"I've had it with sitting on that dumb green rug and playing that dumb colored lollipop game!

"I'm ready for a change."

Mr. Jones put down his muffin and coffee. "Beatrice," he said, "do you think I like my job? I'm tired of running for the 7:45! I'm tired of sitting at that desk and working so hard! I'm tired of laughing at the boss' jokes all day!"

"Doesn't sound so bad to me," said Bea.

Mr. Jones looked thoughtfully at his daughter.

"Beatrice," he said, "WHAT IF we trade places today?"

Bea smiled. "Actually," she said, "that makes perfect sense to me."

And so, after breakfast, Bea put on her father's coat and tie. She looked very important. Mr. Jones put on his sneakers and turned cartwheels for a while. He felt better immediately.

Bea caught the 7:45 with time to spare. She slid onto the empty seat next to her father's business associate and best friend, Harvey Hopkins.

"Morning, Harvey," she said, and then explained that she would be taking her father's place today.

"Well," said Harvey, "today is going to be DREAD-FUL. This afternoon is the deadline for the Crumbly Crackers campaign, and we haven't come up with a thing!"

Bea patted Harvey's hand reassuringly as the train pulled out of the station.

The train reached the city and Bea and Harvey hurried to the Smith Building. They took the elevator to the 42nd floor and walked into Smith & Smith Advertising.

Harvey sent around a memo which read:

> Attention: All Executives
> Please note that Mr. Jones will not be with us today. He is at kindergarten. Bea Jones will be taking his place.

And Bea introduced herself all around.

Meanwhile, Mr. Jones had also arrived safely and soundly at Miss Seymour's kindergarten class. He figured the tallest person in the class was Miss Seymour, and handed her a note which read:

Dear Miss Seymour,

Please excuse Beatrice from class today. She is tired of being a kindergartener. Mr. Jones is taking her place.

Sincerely,

Mr. Jones

"Well," Miss Seymour sputtered, "I must say, this IS rather unusual. But—since I do have a note from the child's father," and she looked over her glasses at Mr. Jones, "I suppose it must be all right with me."

Well, Mr. Jones loved being in kindergarten. He was
a whiz at the colored lollipop game.

"Vermilion red, I believe."

Miss Seymour told him he was almost as bright as
Jimmy Davis, the class genius.

At snacktime, Mr. Jones was chosen as milk and cookie monitor, and he didn't spill a thing.

At recess, he helped Miss Seymour get Jimmy Davis down from the magnolia tree. Miss Seymour told Mr. Jones that he was a big help.

In fact, Mr. Jones was rapidly becoming the teacher's pet. "Oh, Mr. Jones," Miss Seymour sighed, "you're wonderful."

Back at Smith & Smith, Bea was fitting in just fine,
too. The first thing she did was give her secretary the day
off. Then she sharpened all her pencils and drew a nice
picture on her blotter. She was very busy.

At the board meeting, Bea laughed harder than anyone at the boss' jokes. She thought they were great.

"To get to the other side?" Bea chuckled. "That's wonderful!"

Best of all, Bea came up with a wonderful new jingle
for Crumbly Crackers, just in time to save the account.
"Gentlemen, listen to this—
Munchy Crunchy my dear snackers,
You will love our Crumbly Crackers."

"Astounding!"
"A genius!"
That afternoon, Bea was offered a promotion.

When Mr. Jones came to pick Bea up at the train station, they were both very tired, but very happy.

"I feel more relaxed than I have in twenty years!" said Mr. Jones.

"I love advertising! What a challenge!" said Bea.

So, the next day Mr. Jones went to kindergarten and
Bea went to the office once again.
And the next day, and the next, and the next.
At work, Bea was made president of toy sales.

And at kindergarten, Mr. Jones continued to astound Miss Seymour and his classmates with his extraordinary intelligence.

Mr. Jones and Bea had each found their proper niche in the world.

So, remember that big kid you saw getting in for half
price at the movie matinee, and you just couldn't believe
he was under twelve?

Well, you were probably right.

And remember that very short executive that you saw
having lunch with your father last Thursday?

Well, perhaps you know who that was too.